5/1/17 · dugan 1599

GO-GO
gorillas

Julia Durango
Illustrated by Eleanor Taylor

Simon & Schuster Books for Young Readers
New York   London   Toronto   Sydney

E
DURAN

For the Stevenson-Trupiano
gang with gorilla hugs
and gratitude—J. D.

I dedicate this book to Bram—E. T.

SIMON & SCHUSTER BOOKS FOR YOUNG READERS
An imprint of Simon & Schuster Children's Publishing Division
1230 Avenue of the Americas, New York, New York 10020
Text copyright © 2010 by Julia Durango
Illustrations copyright © 2010 by Eleanor Taylor
SIMON & SCHUSTER BOOKS FOR YOUNG READERS is a trademark of Simon & Schuster, Inc.
For information about special discounts for bulk purchases, please contact
Simon & Schuster Special Sales at 1-866-506-1949 or business@simonandschuster.com.
The Simon & Schuster Speakers Bureau can bring authors to your live event.
For more information or to book an event, contact the Simon & Schuster Speakers
Bureau at 1-866-248-3049 or visit our website at www.simonspeakers.com.
Book design by Lucy Ruth Cummins
The text for this book is set in Soup Bone.
The illustrations for this book are rendered in watercolor.
Manufactured in China
10 9 8 7 6 5 4 3 2 1
Library of Congress Cataloging-in-Publication Data
Durango, Julia, 1967–
Go-go gorillas / Julia Durango ; [illustrations by Eleanor Taylor].—1st ed.
p. cm.
Summary: Summoned to the Great Gorilla Villa by King Big Daddy to meet
the newest member of their family, ten gorillas arrive on time using
various forms of transportation, including hot-air balloon, taxicab, and
pogo stick.
ISBN 978-1-4169-3779-1 (hardcover)
[1. Stories in rhyme.
2. Gorilla—Fiction. 3. Transportation—Fiction.]
I. Taylor, Eleanor, 1969– ill. II. Title.
PZ8.3.D933Go 2009
[E]—dc22
2007045160

first edition

In the Great Gorilla Villa,
King Big Daddy paced the floor.

Then he called his royal messenger
and steered her toward the door.
"Summon every last gorilla
to the Villa, don't be late.

I expect them all by sundown—
please don't make Big Daddy wait!"

Go get
gorillas!
Gotta get
gorillas, go!

First to get the message was
Big Daddy's nephew Ike:
"I'll pack a pickle sandwich,
then I'll ride there on my bike."

Niece Isabel was second:
"There's no need for you to worry.
If I row there in my rowboat,
I can make it in a hurry!"

Go-go gorillas!
Gotta go,
gorillas, go!

Third came Aunt Minerva:
"Please relax, my dear," she said.
"If walking isn't fast enough,
I'll roller-skate instead."

Fourth was Uncle Mario:
"I'll drive there in my truck.
I hope it doesn't fall apart—
good-bye, and wish me luck!"

Fifth came sister Flora:
"There's no need for you to fuss.
If I hustle to the station,
I can catch the Villa bus."

Sixth was brother Filmore:
"I can make it in a flash.
I'll just jump in my jalopy—
catch ya later, gotta dash!"

Cuz Clementine was seventh:
"Don't you fret, I'll be there soon.
I can make it if I sail off in my
new hot-air balloon."

Eighth was cousin Cletus,
hopping haywire down the lane.
"I'll bounce there on my pogo stick;
it's quicker than a train."

Go-go gorillas!
Gotta go,
gorillas, go!

Ninth was Grandpa Boris:
"Guess we don't have time to gab.
Catch your breath a moment
while I call a taxicab."

Tenth and last was Granny,
hobbling slowly on her cane,
who told the nervous messenger,
"No sweat, I'll take my plane!"

Go-go gorillas!
Gotta go,
gorillas, go!

The group arrived, all ten,
in time to hear Big Daddy's news.
The messenger sighed happily,

then promptly
took a snooze.

Big Daddy greeted all his kin,
a proud look in his eyes.
"I'm glad you all could come because
I have a big surprise."

Big Mama strutted forward,
in her arms a small gorilla.
"Please join us as we welcome
our new princess . . .

Sweet
Priscilla!

"So gather round, gorillas!
What a party! What a show!
'Cause in the Great Gorilla Villa,
now Priscilla's on the go!"